Long Ago Tales of the Adirondacks

Bradley Luberto

Foreword

The following stories here within are not true.

Some are based on the truth of a myth, as I like to say. Leather Jack, follows somewhat of a true person.

Of Old Hank; when my sister was young, our mother would tell her stories of "Old Hank."

Old Hank was created by our mother, made up, he was and old man that for some reason had gone off to live by himself in a cave. 10 years younger than my sister, by the time I came along Old Hank, was kind of a family legend in story. The stories weren't really told to me as fully as they were to my sister, I being told bits and pieces.

What I was never told was why Old Hank went off to live in a cave. Maybe there wasn't even a real beginning, to these stories, just a fanciful, "Once upon a time, there was an old man who lived in a cave."

Half a century later, I have deiced to give Old Hank a beginning.

I hope my mother would have enjoyed it.

I also dedicate this book to the only thing that is important to me, my wife, Tammy. For without a wife, what good is life?

I also give many thanks to Bernadette Weaver for her endless help in proof reading and friendship.

Copyright 2020

Bradley Luberto

The Leaf

When I was about eight or nine, my parents sent me off to stay with my grandparents for the summer. I didn't know it then, but my mom and dad for a while had been having marriage troubles. They must have wanted some time alone; maybe they didn't want me to hear them fight, which they did as they worked out their problems.

My grandparents, on my mother's side, lived on the outskirts of Macon, Georgia. When I was a kid this was still the rural south. Some of the roads were paved, many were dirt, all had trees hanging down making the roads look more like green tunnels. Grandma and Grandpa's house was on a shady lane; just a dirt road that I can still clearly see.

White fencing ran in front of most of the houses on this road; wildflowers and brambles of every kind worked their way up and through the fencing, bees buzzed from yellow to purple flowers, and the light breezes made the trees seems to sigh with breath.

It wasn't a wide road; two cars could pass each other, maybe coming close to the white fences when they did, but they could pass. It was more a road you'd expect to see a doctor's buggy or fringed top surreys going down.
There were one or two big houses on this road, not plantation big, but large homes that you knew the family was well off, maybe a doctor or lawyer. They were set back on their land, a little hard to see from the road, tall homes with three floors, some with a porch off each level.

Grandpa's house was a small, white house, its front porch also wrapped around one side to a kitchen door. There was a wide wooden porch swing that hung from chains from the porch ceiling, and wooden rockers that cracked with each rock, some chipped green wicker furniture with dusty cushions stood here and there also, one's that Grandma always complained about when the cushions got wet after a rain.

The sun is hot in the south, so much hotter than the sun in upstate New York in the summer. Some days I'd help Grandma in the kitchen; we'd break green beans together making them a smaller size, she said, that's why they call them snap beans because of the snap they make when you break them.

Grandma and Grandpa's house was old. The stove was white and green and on high legs, not like the big six burner stove my mom had back in New York. Grandma didn't have the nice silver pots and pans my mother did, the ones with copper bottoms. Grandma had heavy black pots and pans that she said she always had to dry well and keep seasoned. The refrigerator was kind of rounded, and Grandma had an old pot under what she called the ice box, this was the freezer, that was kind of just a little door at the top center of the refrigerator. She said she kept that pot there, because sometimes on really hot days the ice dripped even in the refrigerator. This too was nothing like the big two door refrigerator my mother had.

Even the sink had a big black pump on it that Grandma said was well water. But she said not to drink that water, that was only now for washing dishes; the sink did have real faucets also.

The rest of the house was old also. The living room was what Grandpa called the parlor and seemed always dark; puffy white curtains hung at its three windows. The furnishings were dark too. The sofa had such a thick flower print that you could feel the stitching of the flowers on it. The arms of the chair were curly also, and I remember having the fun of following the curls with my finger tip.

The bathroom was the oddest one I've ever seen, the toilet had a box high in the air, and to flush it you had to pull a wooden handle that hung down from the box on a chain.

I slept at night in a single bed that had the heaviest sheets that I had ever slept in, and the bed spread was tufted with a fancy design. Grandpa would never let me shut the window of the bedroom at night. He'd say, "the night air is good for you boy. Air keeps you alive!"

Most days by noon it was too hot to do much of anything but sit on the porch. Grandma would sit in one of the green wicker chairs and knit or crochet.

In the corner of the porch up by its wood ceiling hung what looked like a little gray chandelier. Grandpa said it was a paper wasp nest, in each of the little chambers was a baby wasp. He said if you don't bother them, they won't bother you. And they never did! I'd watch the dark brown wasps go to and from the nest. One day Grandpa told me to go look at the nest, it was empty! He took it down for me to see one day. I held the light gray nest in my hand, it was so light, it was like it wasn't even there.

Most of the time Grandpa would sit in a creaking rocker, waving an old gray hat whose faded black ribbon was stained with sweat, before his face to keep a little cool. He'd sit there with an old leather bible in his lap and read it for hours as he rocked. It wasn't a big bible, but it was thick and old; its pages brown, stained by age and noted in places by dark ink from fountain pens.

Grandma and Grandpa were church goers. Every Sunday morning, we would drive off to a small little white church. Cars and cars were parked around it, and everyone seemed to know everyone. Women still wore hats and gloves, not a man was not in a suit. Little girls wore dresses, and some of the young boys wore suit jackets and shorts that matched. I always felt kind of odd, just dressed in dress pants and a clean white long sleeve shirt, but I guess Mom didn't send me to Grandma's with a suit. And I guess as I was only staying for the summer. Grandma did not think there was a need to go out and buy one for me. Most of the time Grandpa seemed to wear a light-colored suit; not white, more of a cream.

The preacher, preached a long service on Sunday. Sometimes when it was really hot in the church, he'd stop the service and say, "I think that it's time for some refreshments."

You could hear a laugh or a sigh, and everyone got up and went outside for a while or to the church kitchen where the women would have large pitchers of ice water on a counter with a stack of little pointed paper cups next to them. There were times I could have drank a whole pitcher of ice water by myself!

When we'd settle back in the pews, the preaching was over and now it was testimonial time and hymn singing. Once Grandma stood up and said how happy she was to have me at her house for the whole summer. I was so proud she said that. I could have cried. I loved to hear the hymns and the piano being played. One or two of the hymns I knew, but most I didn't, but still enjoyed hearing them. Sometimes Grandpa would stand up and sing a song all alone by himself.

Back then I thought Grandpa was old, maybe like 90... but now I know he was about 70. He was thin, bald headed, and tan from the sun. The preacher must have asked if anyone wanted to sing? Grandpa would put his hand up and then stand to sing. For as old as I thought Grandpa was, he had a clear strong voice. I remember him singing once and I can still hear the words, he sang,

I am one of God's sheep

Lost on the mountain,

Lost on the mountain so high.

But God will find me,

He'll come and guide me,

For He will not let me die.

No one ever clapped in church, and it was so quiet when Grandpa had stopped singing and sat back down.

One time after church, Grandpa walked me out back of the church where there was a graveyard. He showed me two stones, tall and white. I don't remember the dates on them or the names, but

Grandpa said that they were his mother and father. Between the two tall stones was a small white stone that had a little white stone lamb on it. I asked him what it was? He only rubbed the top of my head and said, *"Come on, we should be going."*

Sometimes after church, we'd go to town for lunch at a little diner on I guess the main street. It was pretty place, with blue and white curtains at large bright window with people walking by on the street. There was a long counter with a blue top, and shiny silver stools that were fastened to the floor but their tops spun. On the counter were muffins and pies covered with large glass domes. Mostly men seemed to sit at this counter, some were men in bibbed overalls, one with a red handkerchief hanging out of his back pocket.   Other men were dressed nicely; trying to read a newspaper while holding it over their plate of food.

There were tables and chairs also that matched the counter and shiny stools, blue and silver, and families sat at these; men talking to their wives while little kids swung their legs back and forth because they couldn't reach the floor from the chairs, and women fed their babies.

Grandma, Grandpa, and I sat in booths with high backs that were in front of the big windows. The blue seats felt cool to sit upon on hot Sundays. I liked the booth best and it was fun to watch the top of the heads of the people in the next booth moving back and forth at times. It was here at this diner that Grandma reminded me always to say *Thank you, and No thank you ma'am,* and *yes and no sir,* when spoken to.

Fall comes late in the south, later than upstate New York, and I remember when my Mom and Dad came to pick me up and bring me back home with them. Mom had brought a leaf with her, one multi colored leaf of red, brown, and yellow. I liked it. Everything was so green still in the south, never would I have thought the leaves were changing at home.

We stayed that night at Grandma and Grandpa's. I remember falling asleep that night watching the thin curtains that hung in my bedroom sway in the warm southern air. Thunder rumbled almost too faint to hear, and a soft rain started to fall as I fell to sleep.

In the morning after breakfast we said our good byes on the porch. Grandpa was already sitting in a rocker with his bible open on his lap. I kissed him on the cheek and started to walk away, then turned back and said, "This is for you Grandpa." I handed to him the dry leaf my mother had brought for me. He took the leaf from me, set it on a page of his bible and closed it.

Adirondack Joe

Deep in the Adirondacks Mountains, as all my grandfathers' tales began; live a man named Joe, Joe the Skinner as they use to call him, because he did a lot of the taxidermy work for the hunters in the area. He also did some butchering.

This was in the days before the waters of the Sacandaga filled the valley, when steel rails were pinned to hard earth, and roads where only wide enough lean their way to thin wheeled auto. These were the days when sandy paths lead their twisting way through deep and dark pines on roads you could get lost on forever. Farmers plowed the earth into rows, cornstalks stood like golden tee pees in hazy Indian Summer days. While the names of town now long forgotten, were the homes of many.

Gramps said Joe was a tall man well over 6 feet, many say closer to 7. Gramps even had and old picture of Joe, where he got it or who took it, I don't know, I never asked

Gramps, but remember seeing it as a kid.

The picture was an old black and white one, wrinkled some and a little faded, but there was a man standing in it, a real tall man in front of an old log cabin. He was tall, as his shoulders were above the top of the doors frame. The cabin, what could be seen of it looked of rough pine, its roof split wood shingle.

Gramps said he use to go by Joe the Skinner place when he was a kid; a lot of the kids did, Grandpa said.

Joe always had about 6 or 8 deer dressed out and hanging in his yard, bear too. Gramps said sometimes a big bearskin would be nailed right to the side of Joe's cabin. Rabbit, muskrat and beaver were stretched out too in small hoops that looked like shields.

The place, Gramps said always smelled of blood. Even years later after Joe was gone and his cabin had fallen in on its self; Gramps said you could still smell the blood.

Joe was an OK guy until it seems he went crazy, or maybe he always was. It was kind of a local joke whenever someone was missing; people would say, *maybe Joe the skinners got him?* Mothers would scare their kids off to bed by saying, *"Better get to bed or Joe the Skinner will get you!"*

The Adirondacks is some ways is dangerous place. There were always black bear, mountain lion and wolves.

Then too this was during the Depression. Work was pretty steady in the mountains; lumber mills always were running. Loggers always seemed to need help, young men would join a crew for a few weeks, but logging wasn't for the weak.

Easier money could be found in the mills or shops of Gloversville or Johnstown. Rents were fair and jobs were plenty. Then too, some just look for what they thought would be a better life is a big city like Albany or even Manhattan.

So it wasn't that odd if someone would

turn up missing. As time passed it seemed less and less people were hunting. Stores were coming in bring all sorts of foods. Fresh meats could be had as easy as a walk to the butcher.

But taxidermy and butchering was all Joe knew. Joe the Skinner wasn't seen for week's maybe even months at a time. But then this wasn't odd for Joe.   If you didn't go out into those woods to see him for skinning work or a butchering, you might not have seen Joe for months some times.

Gramps said Joe had an old Model T that he would take down to the dry goods store every now and then to buy supplies. Gramps said it never had any license plates on it at all. Gramps said he guess Joe figured he didn't need any as he never left the Adirondacks only went from his cabin to the dry good store and back.

It was some time in the 1940's, one winter that Joe wasn't seen for a very, very long time. The deep snows of the north woods made travel into the Adirondacks difficult at best, even with snowshoes. If there wasn't snow, the unpaved roads were frozen into deeps hard ruts. And when the spring thaw came, they were a sea of deep mud.

As late springtime dried the Adirondacks, the sheriff drove back one day to see Joe. Joe's cabin had faired the winter well. Flowers had sprung up everywhere, yellow Forsythia almost blocked the one small window of the cabin while a huge Pine with low hanging limbs swept the cabins roof in a sleepy kind of way. The door of the cabin was shut, and looked as if it wasn't opened in a long time.

The sheriff, leaned in through the cars window and blew the loud horn of his old back and white squad car, and waited. He expected, he hoped, to see Joe come to the dirty glass of the window and look out. But he didn't.

"Joe?" called out the sheriff. But not a sound came from the cabin except the chatter of squirrels and the tapping of woodpeckers. The sheriff stepped away from his squad car and walked up to the door of the cabin. It wasn't locked, it never was. The sheriff could see that the debris of winter had piled up against the outside of the door, showing it hadn't been opened for a long while. He gave the door a few strong raps with his worn night stick that looked more like a child's baseball bat.

He pushed the brim of his cap up with the tip of the night stick. He saw no footprints other than his own at the door, so he knew no one had been in or out of that cabin for a while. He expected the worse, that being that Joe was dead. He pulled the string that hung through the door, that lifted the wooden latch inside. He pushed the door open and stepped in.

Light filtering in through the small window was enough for him to see that Joe was dead on the floor with one of his butchering knives in his hand, a big old curved knife that most would have called an Injun scalping knife.

What the sheriff didn't expect to see was

the rest of Joe's hobby or past time. Inside the cabin were the mounted deer heads, more than you could count, beaver, rabbit and squirrel pelts were everywhere. Even a red fox stuffed and done up nicely standing on a good size log.

But that wasn't the surprise, it was the bodies, the human bodies Joe was working on that made the sheriffs jaw drop. Ten or twelve done up just as well as any other of Joe's work. Some naked standing in the back of Joe's cabin. Others dressed and sitting at the table as if waiting for coffee and pie. The men dressed in suits; one even wore a stiff straw hat. The women dressed well, and an older one with a full bonnet, a younger one with a pretty dress and blonde hair hanging down in fine curls.

The Adirondack Witch

Of all the stories my grandfather told me of life in the Adirondacks of when he was a boy, probably the one I remember the most was the one he told about an old woman who helped my father; he called her the Adirondack Witch.

My grandfather always said he lived in Kingsboro. Everyone now knows this to be the north east corner of Gloversville today, but one time it was called Kingsboro and that's what Grandpa always called it.

In this corner also, his father had built a log cabin a long, long time ago. When I was young Grandpa would take me on walks out to see it. Even then there wasn't much to be seen of it, just some rotted logs remained in the tall grass that looked more like fallen trees than once a home. At one end there were round stones blackened by smoke that was once a chimney, but now they were just stones thrown on the ground.

Grandpa would show me the lay-out of the cabin that had been his home as a boy. At the rubble stones, "That's where the hearth was ," he'd say and point. He said how his mother cooked, hanging heavy black pots from a crane hook, and cooking meats before its red coals.

A table planed from logs and benches too match "stood here," Grandpa would say, showing with his hands their height and width. "A sleeping loft with straw at the other end of the cabin had a ladder so you could get up into it," Grandpa would say. "During the day, the ladder was hung across the width of the cabin on one of its log beams to give you more room. The loft was warmed only by the circling heat of the fire." Grandpa was proud to tell these stories of life when he was young.

He told of a young sister, a frail thing who slept in a cradle before the fire, but the long, cold winters her little body could not stand. A grave wasn't far from the cabin; yellow flowers still grew upon it, but unless you knew why, it was only a patch of wild flowers that bloomed in the spring.

Grandpa's house today was small with white clapboards, a fireplace too to heat it, and two bed rooms upstairs without any heat at all. Grandpa still had a rope bed when I was a boy. He showed me once how to tighten the ropes and said how that saying of, *sleep tight*, meaning just that, that you would have a good night's sleep on tight ropes.

Grandma was gone, I remember a woman at Grandpa's house; small, wrinkled and gray, or maybe I hope to remember.

My mother was gone also, Dad did not talk about her much, maybe it hurt too much. I don't remember her at all. Dad worked for the mills, and we lived in a small house. He rented rooms upstairs from an older woman, who was mean and never had anything nice to say. Once winter was over, Dad would take me to Grandpa's to live, it was the best part of the year. Spring was beautiful by Grandpa. In Gloversville, in "the city" as Dad would call it, the skies were filled with smoke from the mills, the smell of wood and coal fires burned constantly, they set gray clouds that looked like rain clouds over the city.

Even though Grandpa's house wasn't that far away, it seemed miles and miles. Sometimes we'd walk or sometimes we'd go by wagon, or a friend of Dad's would take us out. Dad would say *"good bye"* and *"listen to your Grandfather,"* and off he'd go back to the rooms above the nasty woman. But by Grandpa it was wonderful.

Sometimes I wouldn't see Dad for weeks, but sometimes he'd come out, sometimes have supper with us, and tell me a story or two as I lie on the rope bed. I always hoped he'd be there in the morning, but he never was.

Grandpa had a garden where most of his food came from, beans grew on long strings, squash grew on the ground, and nothing was better than to go out early in the morning and feel everything damp with dew. Grandpa grew pumpkins too, and as fall came on the pumpkins grew big and orange.

Grandpa had a black cast iron stove in the kitchen that he cooked on; I can still see him lifting the round lids off the stove with a silver wire lifter. Grandpa was a good cook, and if we weren't eating at the small table in the kitchen were would take our food and sitting before the fireplace in the living room. This room was small and dark with a low-ceiling. Grandpa didn't have any electricity, only oil or kerosene lamps. Grandpa played the fiddle. When we finished eating, he'd take the fiddle down, that he kept it on a hook right by the fireplace. He said the warmth was good for it. Grandpa was Scottish and he'd play tunes that I never heard before, some were fun and happy, other sad that just the tune alone could almost make you cry.

I would stay with Grandpa right up until fall and really cold weather came back. I was happy to go back with Dad, but always felt sad when Grandpa would say, "Your Dad's coming for you tomorrow, you're going back to the city." But until that day, life was great.

Grandpa taught me a lot, but most of all I loved to hear his stories of long ago. Grandpa wasn't sure when his father came to the Mohawk Valley, he said they were here a long time ago, a time when you had to watch for Indians when you were out in the woods! Grandpa would tell me all sorts of stories, he told me stories of lumber jacks, hermits and Indians. The story that scared me the most was the story of an old witch, an old witch that lived deep in the forest of the Adirondacks.

"Tell me a story Grandpa," I'd ask. Grandpa would smile, stop playing his fiddle, lock its bow across the fiddle, and say, "Why don't I tell you about the Adirondack Witch! I think Grandpa knew I liked that one best.

"You know," Grandpa would say, "Everyone called her a witch, but she wasn't. Not a mean one like you read about in stories. Sure, she was scary to look at, but she did good."

"Where did she live Grandpa?" I'd ask, although I must have heard the story a hundred times. "She lived out that a way," said Grandpa pointing to the mountains. "You know," said Grandpa, "A lumber-jack would get a hurt, and they'd take him to see the witch! There were no doctors close by back then. Most families did their own doctoring the best they could, but sometimes you'd get a lumber-jack with a deep cut, a bleeder they'd call it, and there was no way you could stop that bleeding. Some would try, and some didn't make it. Others would take them *hurts* to the witch. I remember my own father, your great-grandfather getting hurt one day while out gathering bark, you know they need park to tan hides. I was just a young'n at the time, a little younger than you are now. The men he was working with brought him home to my mother, your great grandmother, in a wagon, they said he was hurt bad. He must have slipped with an axe or a spud knife because he had a terrible cut on his leg. Why you could see the white bone of his leg just as clear as anything. They had tied the leg off above the cut, to slow the bleeding some, but there was no way a cut that deep was going to heal up without some help. They asked your great grandmother what she wanted to do. Then one of the men on the wagon said, what about taking him out to the witch? So that's what they did. My mother didn't want me to stay home alone, you have to remember there wasn't another house around for miles back then, not one you could even see a light in a window at. So, she said, "We'll take the boy with us." Well, we all got in that wagon with my pa, and ma in the back, I was on the seat between the two men driving that wagon, and we made the ride out there in the dark. How the men driving that wagon knew their way in the dark I don't know. I couldn't see a foot in front of me, and could barely see Ma and Pa right in the back, but I could hear Pa, he'd give a moan every now and then as that wagon rocked and tilted. Soon we saw a little glow of a light as if it was a campfire. As we got closer, it was just that, the witch she had a big kettle over a fire hanging from tri-pod in front of her cabin. She was a small little woman, not more than four foot tall and seemed very, very old. Everyone said she was an Indian, I don't know, like I said most just called her the old witch.

She knew something was wrong, no one ever came out to her place unless something was really wrong. She walked with a bad limp but came up to the wagon. My mother pulled back the blanket they had put on Pa so she could see the leg. She told them to bring him into her cabin; it was a small place made of logs, leather covered the only window on the front and the roof was of grass and such. The men carried my Pa, in, and they laid him on what looked like cot, his leg was bleeding badly again probably from the rough ride in the wagon.

Her little cabin was lit by candles and there was a fire in the hearth. Herbs and the like hung from the low beams in great bunches. I asked my Ma if Pa was going to die? She said she didn't know. Then the men who helped Pa started to untie the rope they had put around his leg. Pa let out an awful yell and the old witch stopped them fast. She mixed up some herbs and such in a little bowl, grinding them with some sort of stick. She spread the wound wide that was on Pa's leg, and he let about another moan, but she had to do it. Next, she filled the cut with whatever she had in that little bowl. She pushed it deep in that wound and I could see my Pa grind his teeth and almost cry each time. Then she got out a long thin needle and thread. Later I was told that the thread was horse's tail. She sewed that cut up just as if she was sewing closed a meal sack. The men had to hold Pa down as she stitched it shut. Little by little as she reached then end of that cut the bleeding stopped. She put thick spider's web on top of the wound and bandages it up with some rag strips. A lot of people did this with spider's web, your grandma would do that to me when I got a deep cut, but I never had a cut as deep as my Pa got. Then the men carried Pa back to the wagon and we all made the ride back home. Pa was laid up a long time. I remember after a while the men took Pa back to the witch. Pa could walk now, his leg was getting better, but he didn't walk. The men took Pa back to the witch in a wagon again.

I went with the men this time too, to watch. Well the old witch took a sharp knife and cut the horse tail she had stitched Pa's leg up with and pulled it out just like a thread. Pa had a terrible scar all jagged and long going down his leg, but the wound had healed up. Pa went back to work, back to shedding bark and such, he had to go back to work, there was no one to take care of us other than Pa."

"Alright now," Grandpa would say after he finished one of his stories, "Off to bed with you." I'd give Grandpa a kiss and a hug around his neck and head up the small narrow steps that lead to the second floor. I'd stop and look back and Grandpa sitting there in the yellow glow of the kerosene lamps. He looked so sad sitting there in an old rocker, sometimes with his fiddle still on his lap. I always wondered what he might be thinking about, but never asked.

Leather Jack

The following story of **Leather Jack**, is loosely based on Leather Man; A Hermit of Hudson Valley, New York.

Leather Man; his real name thought to be Jules Bourglay, was born about 1858. He died in 1889 in a cave in Briarcliff, New York, and is buried in Sparta Cemetery in Ossining, New York. Among the items found on him were a small prayer book in French.

For 25 years he walked a 365 mile loop in 30 plus days, going through New York and Connecticut, avoiding large towns and main roads. His leather clothing (hence the name Leather Man) at death is reported to have weighed 60 lbs.

Another story my grandfather told me was a story about Leather Jack. Grandpa befriended Leather Jack when he met him years ago. Grandpa said, he was chopping wood in his yard for winter, when he saw something moving not too far off from the tree line behind his house. Grandpa said he thought at first it was a bear, but it was moving kind of from tree to tree as if it didn't want to be seen. Grandpa said he started to shout to scare it off, if it was a bear, but, that's when he saw it was a man. He said the man started to run a bit, but when Grandpa yelled, *"Hey now, you, stop!"* He said the man stopped. Grandpa knew there were hermits in the woods, there always had been. He said sometimes they would sneak up to a house to steal something they needed. Grandpa said that's why he never left any tools lying about his yard, he always locked them up in a tool shed at night. He said he lost many an axe or hatchet that he left stuck in a stump when he had finished chopping wood, only to find it gone the next morning. But Grandpa said he was never too mad, as he knew how badly some of these old hermits needed a hatch or whatever they might take for life in the deep woods.

Leather Jack just stopped after Grandpa saw him, and called to him, he just stood there. Grandpa said, he guessed Leather Jack was caught other times close to people's homes and must have thought it best just to get tongue lashing or maybe a stick or rock thrown at him than to try and make a run for it. But Grandpa said he walked up to Leather Jack and could see he had a kind look in his eyes, if not a sad look. That's how Grandpa and Leather Jack got to be friends.

Grandpa said he invited Leather Jack into his home for coffee and pie. Leather Jack didn't pass that up.

Grandpa could hear that Leather Jack could only speak a little English, mostly Leather Jack spoke French, or French Canadian. Grandpa knew a few words in French, so they could talk a bit.

Leather Jack was kind of a hermit, but a lot of people knew him. He wasn't the type of hermit who just stayed off in the woods all the time by himself, and lived in a little cabin and was almost never seen. Leather Jack didn't even have a cabin to live in, in the woods, he made his home in caves and such, pretty much what bears denned up in for the winter.

Grandpa asked him once how he kept warm on the cold nights we get in the Adirondacks. Leather Jack said he made a big fire deep inside the caves he planned to sleep in, he said this made the rock walls very hot. Once the fire had died out, he'd go into the cave and keep in warm all night long.

Leather Jack, would come to town now and then when he was on one of his travels. It seemed Leather Jack had some kind of route he always followed; he didn't tell anyone that I know of why he always was walking this route.

Leather Jack was going to be arrested one time for vagrancy, because they said he just drifted from one town to another. And because he didn't have a job. But Leather Jack did have money, he would buy and pay for things at a dry goods store, and such places. But where he came about that money no one knew. No one ever accused him of stealing money from anyone. But because he had money and was walking his route, he was going someplace, even if I might be spending a night or two in the woods outside of town. So, Leather Jack was look on more as a hiker than just an old bum with no place to live.

As I said, a lot of people in the towns he came through, knew Leather Jack. Some of the men would give him smokes, tobacco and such. Some of the women would give him pies and other good foods to eat. Leather Jack would softly say *"Je-vous remercie,"* thank you in French.

Grandpa said, one really cold winter night when it had been raining for like a week, Leather Jack came knocking at Grandpa's door. Grandpa opened the door and there stood Leather Jack soaked with rain, and ice forming on his clothing. Leather Jack must have known he needed help that night being that it was so cold and wet for so long, because Leather Jack never asked anyone for help.

Grandpa invited Leather Jack in too warm himself by the fire, while he heated up some stew that Grandpa had made for supper that night. Leather Jack took off his leather clothing that he always wore. Leather Jacks leather clothing was soaked. Grandpa knew there was no way in the out-of-doors, in winter that, that type of clothing was ever going to dry. It was frozen stiff in some places. Beneath it, Leather Jack had on old, dark, overalls that were dry mostly, and three or four old sweaters of which he took two off and thanked Grandpa for drying them before the fireplace also. Grandpa placed Leather Jacks leather clothing before the fire. He put the heavy leather coat over a high back chair and the pants he hung on another chair. Grandpa said he had to keep turning the chair on which leather clothing hung so they would dry. Even Leather Jacks boots were made of heavy leather, and they too were warming before the fire.

Grandpa said he couldn't believe how heavy Leather Jacks leather clothing was, he said it must have weighted 50 or 60 pounds even when dried. He said it was pieces of leather stitched, and re-stitched over and over making it all so very thick and heavy.

He asked Leather Jack why he wore such heavy clothing? Grandpa said Leather Jack told him how he got the idea from after being attacked by a bear one day.

He told Grandpa it was early one morning before sun up, he was heading along a trail he walked many times. There were a lot of thick brush that was always full of rabbit and deer browsing at it. He set traps there many a time for rabbit. He heard a noise in the brush, but he didn't think much of it, suddenly a bear rushed at him! It was a young bear and kind of small. Leather Jack said, he thinks it wanted the bread and dried sausage he had in his haversack than him. But still, it worked him over good, scratches here and a bite there, but once it broke the cloth strap of the haversack, it took that and ran off back in the brush. That's when he got the idea of making a suit of clothing out of leather. The next time a bear rushed him Leather Jack just pulled his hands back into the wide cuffs of his jacket and pulled his head down deep into the collar of his coat just like a turtle.

He said the next bear was a big one and he was glad he had his new leather suit on. He said that bear came up behind him when he was cooking as night came on. The bear jumped him, and Leather Jack tucked himself in his leather clothing fast. That big bear battered him around good, and he could feel that bears mouth bite down hard on him, but his teeth didn't come through the thick leather.

Grandpa said he asked Leather Jack once why he keep to himself and walked and lived in the woods? He said, Leather Jack showed him a small gold locket he wore on a thin chain around his neck, he opened it, and showed Grandpa the picture inside it. Grandpa said it was of a young woman holding a little baby.

Leather Jack said in his rough English, "Gone, all gone."

Grandpa thought it must have been Leather Jacks wife and baby daughter. Grandpa said he didn't ask Leather Jack much about it again. He said, the few times he did, Leather Jack didn't come by Grandpa's house for months, then he'd start showing up again. But grandpa never asked him again about that locket.

A Night In Nelliston

When we were kids, we grew up hearing the stories of the Mohawk Valley; some were of ghosts and witches, others just about people long ago. It seemed no town was without its own stories, and my grandfather knew a lot of them. He would tell us these stories hour after hour.

Most began "When I was a boy in the Adirondacks." But some weren't "In the Adirondacks," but in the many small towns and villages that were spread out along the Mohawk Valley.

One was about Jacobus Ehle of Nelliston. Grandpa said old Jacobus Ehle was a preacher to both white man and Indian a long time ago in the town of Nelliston.

I guess there was nothing scary about Jacobus Ehle; he was as Grandpa called him, "One of the old folks of the Valley." His house is gone now, all fallen in on itself, even if that much is left today. I haven't been back to it since I was a child.

Grandpa always said one day he was going to take me to Jacobus Ehle's old house; and he did.

It was a little hard to find, but Grandpa knew where it was. He took me to many old places; I think he just liked walking around them. Grandpa liked old things a lot, even his home was filled with old things, old spinning wheels, old butter churns, and what seemed to me when a child just about a hundred old pewter mugs, some with glass bottoms that which I would pretend I was a pirate drinking from it!

We drove out in Grandpa's old model A Ford. I can still hear that old auto all these years later, that motor just had a sound it seemed to go a tic tic tic.

Those were cars back then, it had a soft top like a convertible today, but it didn't have side windows but sheets of isinglass that you had to put on and snap to the top and the doors frame. It was a warm spring day the first time Grandpa took us out there; *us,* is myself and two of the best pals a fellow could have, one was Ed Moss and the other was James Woods, who we always called Jim. It seemed a long drive out from Gloversville, but it was a beautiful spring day the weather warm and the sun bright. It was all dirt roads back then from Gloversville to Nelliston it was all dirt roads just about everywhere!

I loved to take rides with Grandpa he seemed to know everyone and had a story for just about everything too. He'd point out other old homes or where ones once were, or even open fields and say, "That's where Indians made their camp long ago." We'd drive through miles and miles of farm land, it seemed it was either corn fields or pastures of cows flicking their tails at swarms of flies. Every now and then we'd come to a little town, Grandpa would wave to men standing on porches, men wearing light suits and flat top straw hats. Some were farmers in bibbed overalls looking hot and dirty.

There wasn't much of Nelliston back then, as I can remember, there was one store, kind of like a general store, it had wheel barrels standing on its porch out front, a wooden barrel of rakes and shovels, a bench if you wanted to sit, and on the glass of its window were curved red letters that said ice-cream. There was a post office and a few houses. Grandpa turned his car towards the end of the street, and pulled off the dirt road into a field. The minute you got out of the car you could hear bees just buzzing everywhere.

"Come on this way boys" said Grandpa. "I'll show you an old house." We followed Grandpa across a meadow of wild flowers that were waist high, bright blues, yellows and white ones, bees still dancing everywhere from flower to flower.

There didn't seem much of a trail, but Grandpa seemed to know where he was going. Down towards the Mohawk River we headed, we weren't close to it, but even here you could hear the water taking its time rolling along its banks. We turned towards a stand of trees that stood in the meadow. As we came closer, we could see the remains of an old house made of field stone. Its wooden door stood open, it had two windows aside the door that still had wavy panes of glass in them.

"It's still here," said Grandpa walking up to it. It was a small house, maybe 20 feet wide and as deep. Two windows were on the back wall the same as the front. Its flooring was rough timber leveled, kind of smoothed and flattened.

"This is it," said Grandpa, "Old Preacher Ehle's house." Grandpa shut the door, large gaps could be seen all the way around the door, and something had gnawed a large hole in one corner of it. Bright sunshine shone through the back windows, throwing its light on a large fire place that seemed to take up much of one wall. A rusty old bar called a crane hook, hung over the open fire place. Jim swung the bar out; it made a screeching noise. There were no other rooms but this one, the roof reached to a point not too high above Grandpa's head, maybe four feet. Tree branches were nailed to the rafters,

Grandpa said that's where they would have hung foods they were drying for winter. Grandpa reached up and touched one of the many nails that were sticking out of the branches.

"Where did they sleep?" asked Ed Moss looking around. "Probably there," said Grandpa pointing to the wider wall beside the fire place. "They needed to keep the beds as close to the fire as possible to keep warm," He added. "Maybe the young 'ins, slept up there for a while." Grandpa pointed to the rafters at the other end of the small stone house. "There might have been some boards put across from wall to wall, a corn shuck mattress and a feather quilt and you'd be as warm as birds in a nest!"

Ed looked at me with big eyes, it didn't seem like any way he'd like to sleep! "You boys should try it sometime," said Grandpa. "Try it?" I repeated his words. "Sure," said Grandpa. "Spend the night out here, see how the old timers did it." "How would we get out here?" asked Jim. "I'll drive you out," said Grandpa. "I'll come back in the morning, or stay as long as you like."

None of us said anything, but I did think it might be fun.

"Just watch out for the ghost," said Grandpa. "Ghost! said Ed loudly."Full of them out here," said Grandpa. "Why they brought back many of the wounded from the Battle of Stone Arabia here. Patch them up the best they could. But many back then would just die after a battle like that, you know those old muskets. A musket ball didn't make just a little hole in you. No! Why it must have felt like you were kicked by a mule and then some. That round ball would hit your clothing, whatever you had on and just push it deep inside you. Causing a bad infection. And they were fighting Injuns too! Sure, some of them had muskets, but it must have at times got down to some hand to hand fighting. Why the Injuns still carried their tomahawks and knives, and the Injuns were still taking scalps to hang on their belts as a war trophies!"

"Did anyone ever live after being scalped Grandpa?" I asked?

"They sure did," said Grandpa. "Some did any way. But it took a long time for a scalp to grow back and cover that kind of wound, if it did at all. They must have lain them hurt fellow's right here on this floor, the worse off ones anyway. The others must have been outside."

"How do you know there are ghosts Grandpa?" I asked. "I've heard about it," said Grandpa. "Heard the stories. You know that battle was in October, I bet a lot of them spirits show up on Halloween!" "What kind of stories, Grandpa?" I asked again.

"Well I heard people tell of hearing moans and cries coming from this old place. Men yelling *'save my leg, save my leg, don't cut it off!'* You know they didn't set bones like they do today. If a bone was broke and coming through your skin, why they'd just cut your leg or arm off about where the bone was poking through."

"Didn't it bleed?" asked Jim. "Sure it did," said Grandpa. "But they'd cauterize it." Jim just looked at Grandpa. "Burn the end of the stump with a hot knife or something like that. Probably heated it up right in that fireplace too." Grandpa pointed to the hearth , then said, "Bandage it up with some cloth and you were good to go." "Go where?" said Ed. Grandpa laughed.

"You boys should come out maybe in the fall, see if you see or hear anything. Come on," said Grandpa "Let's have a look around."

We walked outside, back of the small house. Ed pulled at my shirt sleeve as we began walking, "You know," said Ed, "If we do, do this overnight thing, I think I'd rather do it in the fall. No spiders. Did you see the size of the hoop webs in there?" I nodded yes. Ed put his hands up showing their size. "Like two feet across!" he said. "I think getting hit by a musket ball might be better than getting bit by one of them," he added.

Behind the house was an old well, its round wall standing about waist high. Some rotting boards where set across it. Grandpa pushed the boards aside. "Still water in it," he said. "You boys come out you won't have to bring water, this well is fine." The three of us looked down into the deep well, clear cool water reflected the blue sky above us.

Grandpa slid the board back over the well. "Come on this way," said he as he walked on. "This is an apple tree," said Grandpa patting a large tree. "If the deer don't get it all you'll have food too!" Grandpa seemed certain that we were going to do this overnight thing come fall. A little further on a small stream snaked its way along, no doubt leading down to the Mohawk. The sun was getting hot now. I put my face up to its light.

"Come on," said Grandpa again. "We'll head back, but first I'll buy you boys some ice-cream in town."

Spring shortly turned to summer, and all summer long we talked about asking my grandfather to take us out to Nelliston, to Jacobus Ehle's house so we could stay a few days. We knew Grandpa would do it, do it any time for us. But we also thought what fun it would be to do in October when it was cooler, when the battle of Stone Arabia did occur, and there wouldn't be any spiders!

Fall came on as only it can in the Adirondacks; it isn't brilliant, but warm with colors, the green pines that never change soften the colors to a glow. Yes, sharp contrast, but not an endless running of color. Coal and wood fires start to fill the air too with their scents, and there is always someone burning leaves. And when cornstalk and pumpkin adorn almost every home, and bouncing crepe paper, goblins appear in doors, you know Halloween is near.

It was week before Halloween when I said, "Grandpa, you still want to take the fellows and I out to Jacobus Ehle house?" "Wondered when you boys were going to get around to doing that," said Grandpa.

I told Grandpa we thought of going out Friday, about mid-day, and then he could come and get us Saturday about the same time, if that was OK? Grandpa said that was a good time, as it would give us *settle in time,* as he called it. He said, we'd need lots of fire wood even for one night.

It was set, we'd take our heaviest blankets, roll them up trump-line style, canned foods, bread and coffee. Jim was a boy scout, he had everything we'd need. He even had a nesting cook kit with a small kettle.

Grandpa said to come over to his house about noon and he would drive us all out. He kind of joked but I think he meant it, saying *I thought you boys would want to stay for a week!"*

Friday afternoon was a perfect fall day, bright clear crisp, leaves fell with each gust of wind. We all met at Grandpa's house it was only blocks from our homes. Grandpa came out to find us all on his porch; blankets rolled and knapsacks full. "All set?" asked Grandpa. We all nodded yes. "Well into the car then," he said.

The ride out was the best ever, Grandpa told endless stories. At Nelliston, Grandpa parked his car about the same place he did when he first took us out there. "Ck," he said. "I'll walk with you a way until we come to the house." "That will be good Grandpa," I said while thinking, I hope the house is still standing!

The flowers of spring were gone, brown dried weeds reached to our waist and strong red vines grabbed at our shoes. We turned towards the stand of trees in the meadow, there were few pines, but the trees about the small house were nearly leafless. The door was again open, it looked more inviting in the spring I thought. The window panes were dusty and the house just looked dark.

"OK boys," said Grandpa. "Only one night, you're sure?" Grandpa patted the old home. "One-night Grandpa," I said giving him a hug.

I had set my knapsack down; it was a tan

boy scout one that Jim and let me use. Grandpa picked it up one handed by its two straps. "What do you have in there boy?" he asked. "It feels like you have enough food for a month!"

He set it back down giving each of us a pat on a shoulder, then turned and walk away. I saw him pull a white handkerchief from his back pocket and wipe his eyes. I don't think he was sad he wasn't staying; I think he just missed us already.

All three of us just stood before the small house and looked at it. The sky in Gloversville was bright and sunny, here in Nelliston it was starting to turn gray, silver clouds were filing the blue sky.

"Well," said Ed. "I think we should get these packs inside and then get a good load of wood. I don't think it's going to rain, but it might get cold." The little house didn't weather the spring and summer well, a lot of dust and dirt seemed to cover the floor, besides the dusty window panes, there even seemed to be a few holes in the roof, or maybe we just didn't notice them before. But the spider webs were gone!

We stacked our knapsacks on the floor with our bed rolls on top to keep them clean for the moment.

"OK," said Ed, "let's get that fire wood." There were lots of fallen limbs about, Jim had brought his hatchet and was chopping some of the large limbs up, but most were small enough to just snap. "You use a lot of wood on a fire," said Jim. "More than you'd think." "Besides, we might want to stay another night!" Jim said. Both Ed and I looked at Jim, we knew he was joking and besides we had no way of letting Grandpa know not to come get us if we planned to stay. Arms full of wood we carried it all into the small house stacking it by the fireplace. Jim swung the crane hook, again it made the same screeching noise.

"We can hang our pots from here," said Jim. "I have a little fire grate but we won't have to use it." The wind picked up again, a strong wind that even blew the arms of the leafless trees.

"Hey, you think there's any apples left or did the deer eat them all?" asked Ed. There wasn't much left of the apples that was for sure, a lot of rotted ones on the ground, but there were still a few good ones on the tree. We rubbed our apples on our sleeves as we walked around a little while eating them. Not far from the house old stones walls seemed to just run into the woods. We walked atop them balancing ourselves as we did.

"Hey, where do you think they buried their dead? You think there is a graveyard around here? What about the soldiers that must have died here?" asked Jim. "You think they buried them here too?" Colored leaves lay thickly across the ground and scattered over the long stone walls, if there was a graveyard it could be anyplace, but not a tombstone seemed to stand anywhere.

We pulled our wool jackets tighter around us. "Maybe we should have worn heavy clothing," I said feeling the cold suddenly.

"We'll be fine" said Jim. "Once we get a hot meal in us and a fire going. You'll see."

The Mohawk River seemed to be louder than it was in the spring too, maybe because there were less leaves on the trees. We couldn't see the river from the house, thicker pines stood towards the river, and we didn't want to walk that far.

"What time do you think it is?" I asked. Ed, pulled a gold pocket watch from his pocket. "Just past four," he said. "Wow," said Jim. "Time passed fast. Maybe we should get that fire going and eat it will be getting dark soon."

"We'll need water" said Ed. "I'll be right back," said Jim running off towards the stone house. In a few minutes he returned walking over to the old well. "Take the boards off," said Jim as he let a roll of course twine fall to the ground, he tied one end to the bail handle of a small cook pot. I just smiled, Jim was a natural scout he had everything and knew how to use it.

Jim picked up a small smooth rock, he wiped it off in his hands and then set it in the small pot. He lowered the little pot down into the dark well, it sank into the water. "Why did you put a rock in it?" asked Ed. "The pot would have been too light and never sank into the water," said Jim. Ed nodded it made sense. It was this type of thinking that made Jim a true scout.

Jim pulled the twine and brought the little pot back up. Setting this one on the stone edge of the well, he took another pot from his mess kit and poured the water into it. He then lowered the pot again down into the well. "This one's for our coffee tonight," he said, as he then pulled the second full pot of water up.

Back inside the small stone house we started to unpack our knapsacks. Jim filled the small coffee pot with the water from the second pot, putting some coffee in, and set it aside.

"I'll get a fire going," said Jim as he kneeled at the hearth. He gathered some tinder, set larger twigs over that and still bigger wood above that. Jim then stuck a match on the stone hearth but before he could get the match to the tinder, the match went out. Jim stuck another match and again it went out in his fingers. At the third match he lit the tinder.

"I didn't even feel a breeze," I said as Jim sat back a moment to fan the fire slowly. Smoke went up the ancient chimney. "I did," said Jim. "It was like someone was blowing it out in my hand!"

"Ghost!" said Ed.

Jim laughed as he took next out of the knapsack more of his tin cook kit. In a few minutes cans of food were open bread was sliced, and the little house felt like a home.

Jim had hung the small pot of his cook kit from the crane hook. In a few minutes he was spooning out hot soup into tin bowls. The tin bowls were almost too hot to hold from the hot soup , but at the same time the heat felt good on cold hands. I reached for a spoon out of Jim's cook kit, saying, "I think my grandpa would have like to stayed with us."

Ed nodded. "Maybe next time he can." "You wouldn't mind would you Jim?" I asked. Jim shook his head no, with a face saying he wouldn't care.

Suddenly the wooden door swung open with a bang making us all jump. I got up and went to the door. "Not much of a way we can keep this shut," I said swinging it freely back and forth on its hinges.

"We can put a rock outside the door and another inside," said Ed. "It will kind of keep it closed." "Unless someone really wants to come in or just comes in through this hole," I said, putting the toe of my shoe through the hole that seemed gnawed even large at the base of the door. I stepped outside found two rocks and came back in. I opened the door set one of the rocks outside the door's sill, closed the door and set the other rock against the door. I wiggled it back and forth, it thumped against both rocks but seemed as if it would do.

As the fire burned down, Jim put more wood on it and brought the house back to light. "Better keep that going all night," said Ed. "You afraid?" asked Jim teasing. Ed said nothing only wiped his tin bowl clean with a rag he had in his knapsack. "I'll help you clean up," was all he said.

Jim packed up the tin pot he had heated the soup in as Ed wiped the tin bowls clean. Into the hot wood embers Jim set the small pot for coffee. Soon it perked up into the small glass top filling the house with a good scent. Jim's mess kit even had small tin cups of which he handed one to each of us. "Here's some sugar," he said setting a small white cloth bag on the floor. Suddenly the small sack fell on its side.

"How did that happen?" said Jim quickly grabbing it "I thought I set it down flat?" He handed the sack to me, and I shook some of the sugar into my coffee, I then handed the sack to Ed. "Why did you tie it shut?" asked Ed sounding annoyed.

"What?" I said looking to Ed. "The sugar," said Ed. "Why did you tie it shut before handing it to me?" Ed held the small sack out to me in his hand, it was tied tightly closed.

"I didn't tie it shut, I just used it and then handed it to you." Ed said nothing, he untied the bag and shook some sugar into his coffee and took a sip. "It's cold," he said. "Cold!" said Jim. "I just poured it. I can't even hold onto my cup it's so hot. How can yours be cold?" Ed in a growing anger held the cup out for both Jim and I to feel, it was indeed cold. "That's odd," said Jim. "Give it to me and I'll just warm it up on the coals." Ed handed the tin cup to Jim who set it close to the hot embers of the fire.

Again, the door thumped back and forth between the two rocks. "It doesn't even sound like the wind is blowing that hard," I said, getting up and going to the door. I pulled the door open; no wind was blowing. I looked back and Jim and Ed. "Maybe what ever made that hole wants to come back in but can't fit in anymore."

said Ed.

I fitted the rocks tighter to the door pushing on it with my foot. I walked over to Jim and Ed and picked my bed roll. "Turning in?" asked Ed. "No," I said. "Just getting kind of cold. You wonder how these old timers did it, no heat other than that fire place."

In time Ed pulled his watch out again and looked at its face, "Just about nine," he said. "Well maybe I will go to bed then," I said pulling the wool blanket over me as I stretched out on the wood floor. "Probably about that time too," said Ed reaching for his bed roll. "Toss me mine will you?" asked Jim.

Jim caught the bedroll that Ed tossed to him. Jim unrolled it on the floor. He then got up and took from his knapsack a small candle and walked over to one of the windows on the front wall of the house, he lit its wick, dripped a little wax on to the wide wooden widow frame and stuck the lit candle to it.
"Why?" asked Ed. "Why not?" said Jim.

Suddenly the candle went out. "How?" began Jim. "There are so many drafts in this old place." I said. "Nothing going to stay lit long."

Jim shook his head, saying, "Something odd is going on here tonight. Sugar falls, then ties itself shut, hot coffee gets cold fast." Just then the door banged again. "And that!" said Jim. Jim struck another match on the old house and lit the candle.

We lay with our feet towards the fire hoping to keep them warm. I tucked the blanket beneath me the best I could trying to keep some of the cold from the floor coming up to me. The door thumped back and forth between the two rocks, I shook my head, then pulled my head lower into the blanket.

I awoke not sure at what time it was, the fire was out and so was the small candle in the window. Something woke me, I was not sure what, but something woke me. I looked about the dark house I could see nothing. I turned to look up at the roof to see if I could see anything of the sky though the holes. Something swayed back and forth blocking the holes in the roof. Tree limbs I thought, but as I lie there I thought, the apple tree is the only tree close by but it's not that close and not over the roof! The other trees were even further. I struggled to see in the dark. I watched the hole appear and reappear, what was blocking them at times? It was then I saw something, something, more of a shape, it was a man!

"Jim, Jim, Jim, Ed, Ed, Ed." I shouted kicking myself out of my blanket. "There's someone here!" I shouted again. I hit into Ed who was on my right side. "What, what? " Ed was shouting. "What's that?" shouted Jim as he too kicked himself away from the dark figure. "It's a man!" said Ed.

"Where can I put my wounded?" he asked. "May I bring them in here?" he asked. Jim stuck a match on the stone wall of the house, our faces showed before the match, but the man who stood before us did not, in fact the light of the match shown through him onto the wall behind him.

"The battle did not go well," he said. "I've many wounded, myself included." He moved his hand away from his stomach, a dark blotch seemed to hang in mid-air his hand was dark too. "There are many," he said as he slowly faded into the darkness. Jim's match went out in his fingertips. "What was that?" asked Ed. "I don't know," I said standing. The three of us ran to the door, kicked the rocks away and walked out the door a few steps. Before us in the dark, in the weak moon light was a retreating army of men. Wounded and bandaged the best they could be, marching before us. But we could see through them, the brush behind them, trees further on. Every now and then a man on a horse would gallop by saying "There is water up a head, just a little further men, and we can rest."

In silence we watched as these men slowly passed by, disappearing into the darkness of the night and the woods.
The three of us looked at each other, we couldn't all have dreamed this? Maybe

one of us is dreaming? Maybe the other two right now are sound asleep on the floor. Maybe we're all sound asleep on the floor! We turned and walked back into the small house, our blankets askew on the floor, kicked in our haste of getting up.

As mid-day came Grandpa found us waiting where he had parked his car the day before when he dropped us off. We sat there upon our rolled bedrolls.

Grandpa turned his car about on the dirt road and pulled next to us. He looked at us from behind the steering wheel and said " You boys look as if you've seen a ghost!"

Uncle Ray

Of all the haunted stores and ghostly happening in the Adirondacks that my grandfather told me, probably none was more eerier than one that happened to his own family, and on Halloween night!

It happened long ago when my grandfather was a boy. One of his uncles, Uncle Ray, was dying of consumption what today is called TB. Uncle Ray's mother was grandpa's mother's sister, both she and her husband had died. Grandpa never said how, but Uncle Ray came to live with his mother and father after that.

Uncle Ray was always *a sickly child,* as Grandpa would say his mother would say of him, thin, pale, and weak. Didn't enjoy the Adirondacks as other children did. Or maybe he was just too ill to enjoy them.

Grandpa said he remembered Uncle Ray mostly sitting on the porch of the cabin his parents lived in with a blanket over his legs, Grandpa said they tried to *give him as much sun as possible.*

The house, Grandpa said, was never much of a house, not like houses of today. Grandpa said his father had built it of hewn logs, it had no running water, and no electricity ever! A real log cabin it was. But it was home to Grandpa and his brothers and sisters. There was a sleeping loft with a large window for the three boys. No bed to speak of, what was a mattress, was only a large canvas bag filled with straw, hay and dried leaves of corn stalks. The pillows were stuffed the same way, but were just old flour sacks. I'm guessing the mattress was pretty big for three boys to sleep on.

A ladder came down from the loft, that every day was hung on tree nails across the center beam of the cabin to give more room.

The "girls," the two sisters, had a room just below the loft. It wasn't much of a room, it had a wide rope bed, no window, and an old sheet hung from the same beam the ladder hung from in the day time, that give them some kind of privacy. The brothers and sisters would talk through the wide plank flooring of the loft late into the night, until their mother or father trying to sleep in a rope bed next to the stone fireplace would yell out, *"OK kids, knock it off and go to sleep!"* Of course, giggling would continue on until another warning of, *"go to sleep!"* would follow.

When uncle Ray came to live with them, they made a small bed for him next to the fireplace opposite grandpa's, Ma and Pa's bed. I guess they thought that would be a nice warm place for him.

One night they heard Uncle Ray talking away. Grandpa said he, and his brothers were already in bed in the loft, it wasn't that late at night, but night came early in the Adirondacks, no electric meant only candles or kerosene lamps. The "boys," peered over the loft to see what all the talking was about, and the "girls" were peeking out from behind the gray sheeting.

Grandpa could see the kerosene lamp was lit on the worn rectangle table, and that his ma and pa were up and talking with Uncle Ray. Uncle Ray was sitting up in his bed, his back against a sagging pillow. He had a smile on his face and seemed to be talking with someone other than grandpas, Ma and Pa.

Grandpa said, *us kids*, that was he, his brothers and sisters, had all gotten out of their beds now, and were standing on the wide plank flooring of the cabin, just looking at Uncle Ray.

Grandpa said his Pa had an old corn cob pipe in hand as he just stood there looking at Uncle Ray. Ma, was sitting beside Uncle Ray trying to talk with him. Grandpa said he could hear Uncle Ray saying, "*but look, its maw and paw, and its granny too! Right there, right there!* He said, almost shouting.

Grandpa said, Uncle Ray went on to say how there were uncles and aunts and friend there, all telling him, *to come with them now.*

Grandpa said he could hear his mother saying, *"But where are they Roy? Where? I don't see anyone, and where do they want you to go?"*

Grandpa said, Uncle Ray seemed to never look at anyone just to whomever he was talking with. We could see him smiling and hear him laughing like he never did. Suddenly he said, *"I'll come. I'll come with you. Sure, I will."*

Grandpa said he saw Uncle Ray sit up in bed, raise the covers over him a bit like he was going to get up, and then suddenly, he just leaned back against the pillow and was dead.

Grandpa said his ma just cried and cried, while his pa just lit his pipe. Grandpa said that's when his ma turned to his pa and said, *"It's the devils' night, it's Halloween!"* And sure enough it was. It was Halloween. We had forgotten all about that. Grandpa said they never did nothing likes kids do today, no trick or treat'n in the Adirondacks, not in the back woods where they all lived.

Grandpa said his pa, made Ma go back to bed, then he just pulled the covers up and over uncle Ray. Then he sent all us *"young-ins"* back to bed too. There was no more talking or giggling that night.

Grandpa said they all woke up early that morning, earlier than usual. His ma and pa were up. Uncle Ray lie on his bed, his face never looked more whiter. Ma or Pa had stitched up the bed covering around him that only his face still showed.

Grandpa said his father had dug a grave out in what he called the graveyard. Grandpa's, Grandma and Grandfather were buried there, and probably was their too. Grandpa said there were *a mess of babies buried there also.* Grandpa said, so many babies died young, that many didn't *feel the loss,* as people do today. Grandpa said there was never any markers out there, you just knew who was buried where.

Grandpa said his pa had dug a grave for uncle Ray already, maybe he did it in the morning, maybe in the middle of the night, after they all went back to bed some. Grandpa said it was the first burial he had seen there in the family graveyard. He said his ma and pa and his brothers and sisters just stood and watched. He said his pa carried Uncle Ray out and then laid him in that grave, no coffin nothing, just in the bedding they stitched around him.

Grandpa said his ma was crying a bit, and Pa said a few words to the Lord. Then they all just went back to the cabin, and as we did, we could hear that shovel as Pa filled that grave in.

Scalper's Ville

To the north, in the great Adirondack Mountains, 200 hundred years before there was an Adirondack Park, there was what was best forgotten by time and man, a town that came to be called Scalper's Ville.

Prior to its vile name, it was known as Jenkins Ville and before that Jenkins Patten. Deeded to by the King of England, and bartered from the Indians, Jenkins Ville was the home of free-thinking Scotsmen and Germans seeking a life new life.

The large lake called Jenkins Lake was dammed, an over shoot waterwheel were set to run a mill for lumber. Houses were built that turned into homes, and gardens planted. Trees were felled to clear land for planting; the ground broke by steel plow pulled by horse and even human at times. The rocks moved, and stones set as fencing, and soon fields of head high maize were grown.

Village and family grew. Five houses of one room formed the village that first winter; by the winter, of next, 25 homes stood.

The Indians were cautious friends, trading furs for steel hatchets and knives, and the strong drink the men made from their maize.

Today Scalper's Ville is a broad meadow ringed by trees. A few stone walls crisscross the forest floor as does the same pattern in thousands of forests in New England states, of farms long forgotten as families moved on.

Trees, a hundred plus years old, have regrown, splitting the old stone walls turning them back into so much rubble. But, if one knows where to look, crude foundations of homes can be found, in what looks like just a meadow, a village of a few streets would be seen. In every home a hearth stood, scratch at the hard soil and with luck a thick cook pot with studded feet might be found.

At village center near a common green stood, a church in which long sermons were preached repenting of continuous sin and thanks given for the bounty of the land.

Search more, and the blackened charred earth of a smithy's shop will be found, as well as a pitted steel beam set between a channel of rock that once held a proud wheel.

This was Jenkins Ville!

But what turned that night into a torrent of death, none living know. As night came on shots were heard from vigilant guards that stood watch. The forest moved with unsuspecting death.

By morning every member of Jenkins Ville was tied to a stake of wood, and every member, woman or man, young or old was scalped. Fully scalped in the most hideous fashion from hairline to the base of the skull, pulled and cut. Mothers with

blood filled eyes watched as their children
from the youngest of days were scalped
the same way, fine thin hairs on patches of
light skin. The women were robbed of
their decency, their breast tore and cut
asunder. The men mutilated beyond the
recognition of men.

It was a peddler of tinware who found
them, weeks or months later. It was a sight
no mind could recover from.

The wolves had moved in, and very well
their own dogs, loyal pets until the end,
but now changed by hunger also.

The peddler's words brought armed men,
but to whom and to where to follow?

Little flesh was found to bury and the
bones were set to blaze. Evermore to
        be called Scalper's Ville.

Snake Catcher

When I was a boy, my grandfather would tell me stories of when he was a child in Gloversville, in the Kingsboro section of the city.

One story he would tell, was about a man they called the Snake Catcher. Maybe there were a lot of snakes in old Gloversville back then, but when I was a boy visiting Grandpa, playing and running in the woods, I never saw any, maybe the Snake Catcher caught them all?

Grandpa said, the snake catcher name was Old John. Grandpa said, later, he figured Old John, wasn't really that old, maybe no more than 45 or 50. But to Grandpa, when he was a child, Old John seemed old, maybe 90, or even 100!

Grandpa, would tell me how he looked, he said Old John, wasn't a tall man, but wasn't short either, but said he had long gray hair and a beard that matched.

Grandpa said, from time to time, Old John would come to Kingsboro, on his way to Gloversville, to buy supplies and such. And far as anyone knew, said Grandpa, Old John, lived all his life alone in the woods, in not much of a cabin or shack either, just kind of a house of sticks.

What Old John did with the snakes, and why he caught them, no one seemed to know, but Grandpa said, he probably ate them. Grandpa said, he knew people who did. He said, they would say, the bigger and fatter they were, from eating field mice and birds and frogs, the better they tasted.

Grandpa said, Old John, would come down out of the woods into Kingsboro, carrying an old sack in one hand and a long pole his, *snake catching pole*, is what Old John called it, in the other hand. It was about 6 feet long, and had a Y or fork at one end.

Grandpa, said Old John showed him once how he caught snakes. Old John, was like that, good natured, and friendly to all.

Grandpa, said when he was young and Old John would be walking through Kingsboro, and he and all the other kids would run up to Old John to talk with him, and follow him some. They'd asked him how he caught snakes?

Old John once said, he'd show them. Old John went looking about some rock-wall that was all falling down. Old John said there always seemed to be a snake hiding about in rubble like that.

He poked about the dry leaves and grass with his long pole, and lifted a large stone, when suddenly a snake darted out, slithering away in the grass. Old John, took that forked pole, and trapped the snakes head down under that Y. He then pulled an old worn knife that hung from a sheath at his belt, and cut the snakes head right off! The snakes body flipped and turned, and rolled about on the ground. Old John, warned us not to touch the head because even though it was off the snake's body, it still had the *hate in it,* as Old John put it. And that the head would still bite you!

When the snake stopped moving, Old John picked up the body, and held it out so we could see it and touch it, it must have been 4 feet long. He opened the sack he carried, and put the dead snake in it. After that he gave the head of the snake, a good kick with his boot, and sent it flying into the field.

Grandpa said, Old John's clothing looked more like he was a charcoal burner, these were the men who made charcoal. They'd cut and stack wood into a big pile, then cover it with soil. After that they set the wood on fire and let it burn real slow, they didn't want it to burn all up like a campfire, but burn slowly, and turn into charcoal. It's a dangerous and dirty job.

Old John, wore an oversize tweed jacket. He had on bibbed overalls, that both straps over his shoulders were gone, that he had replaced with rope. And for shoes, he had on heavy boots. On his legs below his knees, he wore thick laced leather gators, he made to block the strikes of snakes to his lower legs. On his head, he wore a wide brimmed hat that was pinned up in front with along hawthorn needle.

I asked Grandpa once where Old John lived? Grandpa said, one time when Old John had come to Gloversville, he took a fall and hurt his leg. The doctor wanted Old John to spend a few days in the city, to make sure he was going to be alright. The doctor even said, he could spend a few days at his home, or they would even put him up in a hotel in the city. But Old John would have no part of it. Old John live up in Bleecker Mountain, and that is where he was walking back to, hurt or not. Grandpa said, he and his father were in the city that day, and his father had a car, a model T and he offered to give Old John a ride back home. Grandpa said Old John was not much happier being in an auto, as staying in the city, as he had never been in and auto before.   But Grandpa said, he guess Old John knew how far of a walk it was on a good day and not hurt, then to walk all that way when hurting, so he let them take him back up to Bleecker Mountain by auto.

The roads were all dirt back then, even in

the city, and Bleecker, was nothing more than a mill town, a church or two, and a dry goods store. Once they got up to Bleecker, Grandpa's dad, had to turn down a dirt road that was more like a game trail, the brush and brambles aside the road was swatting the auto as it went along. Old John told them to stop, that his home was *off that way,* as Old John put it. Grandpa said, that there was even less of a trail, the way Old John pointed, little more than a rabbit path as Grandpa put it.

Grandpa said, he told Old John, that he didn't want him walking alone through that, that, we would go with him. Old John tried to say no, but Grandpa said Dad was persistent, so Old John just said okay. The walk from where they park the auto aside that little road, to Old Johns home, it was about a half mile back. What Grandpa and his dad saw really shocked them, Old Johns home, wasn't a cabin, it wasn't even a shack, it was a house of sticks! I guess more like an Indian wigwam.

Grandpa said it was tied together, with string and leather, some skins covered parts of it, and its door, its door was no more than sticks tired this way and then making a flat sheet. They helped Old John into this hut. Grandpa said it was dark mostly, a little light came through the sticks here and there, and the floor was just dirt. On the floor, was a little bed made of sticks and a few small logs kept it off the ground. On it were some furs hides for blankets. A few candles stood on wooden boxes, and there was a barrel with a dipper holding rain water, and that was all there was about.

Grandpa said they made Old John as comfortable as possible, but even at that he didn't want much help, but to be left alone. Grandpa said, he always wondered how Old John made it through the winters on Bleecker Mountain in that little hut. But always seemed to.

Old Hank

If your grandparents or
great-grandparents, grew up around
Speculator, New York, they probably
knew of, or heard stories of an old hermit
and guide, by the name of named French
Louie.

But there was another old hermit around
Speculator, one that my grandfather told
me stories about.

His story went like this.

Far back, and up in the hills of the
Adirondack Mountains, lived Old Hank.
Everyone knew of Old Hank, but few
knew Old Hank.

Old Hanks parents, were Maria and
William, but he was always called Hank.
Old Hank, was really a third, but no one
used such fancy name calling in the
Adirondacks, Junior, was the best he'd get
at times, next to Hank.

Old Hanks father, was a logger, cutting timber for any mill, in any season that was hiring. Hank, could remember seeing his father heading off to work with snowshoes strapped to his back, and with thick bear fur mittens on. He'd wave back to his son, before he was out of sight.

They were times William wasn't home for weeks, sometimes months at a time, it depended on how far back, and how much wood a mill needed cut. William, would come home with stories to tell his son, stories of hauling logs with teams of horses, logs as big around as he was tall, and his arms out stretched. How, they would send them down to the river, and how the river would be so full of logs, you could walk across it on them, and never get wet!

There was a sister too, Ginny; pretty and thin, with blonde hair. She wasn't made for Adirondack life. Keeping chickens for eggs, rabbits for meat, and a cow too, for milk in the early morning, wasn't a life for Ginny.

One of the mill workers, a young man named Sam, liked Ginny a lot. Both William and Maria, didn't like him much. He wasn't like the other mill hands. He worked, but he wasn't *a hard worker,* as William would put it.

A week, if that long after pay day, he was always looking for, *a little cash, just to tied him over to pay day.* He talked a lot about going to *the big city,* New York City, or Boston. He even talked of places out west. He often said, *where a man can make himself rich!*

Ginny, started to like him too. She started saying how much she hated the Adirondacks. And how, *this wasn't living, and she wasn't going to die a mill hands wife!*

One day, Ginny didn't get up for breakfast. Didn't gather the eggs, or milk the cow either. Maria, thought her daughter might be ill so she let her sleep in, and she did her chores. But when 5 AM passed, and then 6, Maria knew she had better check on the girl. Maria opened the door to Ginny's bedroom. The patch work quilt that Ginny so loved, that her mother had made for her when she was 12, covered the thick feather mattress that hung limply on the rope bed. Pinned to the quilt was a note of yellow paper, on it was written in dark ink, *I miss none of you.*

Ginny was gone, and Sam, didn't show up for work any longer either. Hank, loved the Adirondacks, the green mountains, the streams and ponds, and fields of wild flowers was home to him. Whereas his sister, wanted what the world could offer. Hank had what the world could give.

Maybe it was his grandfather, also named William, who had taught Hank what counted most in life. His grandfather said, he only left the Adirondacks once in his life, when a call went up for men to form the 115th Regiment, sometimes call the Mohawk Brigade.

When he came back, he, William, married Grandma, of whom Hank never knew. William, built the little house of three rooms, a home for he and his bride. In time their only child William was born, and in more time, William brought Maria his bride, home to live. Grandma had died that cold winter, and Grandfather, when Hank was 10. But in those 10 years his grandfather taught him all a man needed to know of the woods. If lost in the winter, he knew how to build a snow shelter. He knew what berries to eat, and could bring down a bird or squirrel with a slingshot.

Grandpa and Grandma's graves, were not far from the small home, unmarked, and like their very lives lived, will be forgotten in time. Again, a cry for men when up, and it was Hank this time who answered that call.

From Speculator he left, a hand shake from a red eye father, and kiss to his mother's damp cheek. Hanks mother died while he was in France, and after he came home, Hank was a different man.

Hank, hung his helmet on a nail in the barn, and never taken from that nail again. Hank, began working for the mills as his father did. Then one day, men from the mill came looking for him. His father had been killed, crushed to death by a huge log that had rolled off a truck.

Hanks father was buried in a graveyard beside the church in Speculator. A few men from the mill came, and a few friends from town. After that, Hank moved from the small farm and house his grandfather had built. He moved deep into the Adirondacks, to a cave his grandfather had shown him when we was a boy. Old Hank, moved what furniture he thought he might use to the cave. He took the old rope bed of his sister's that was stored up on the rafter of the barn, its roping gone to mice and time, and what was left fell apart like brittle braids in his hands. The large cast iron cook stove, his mother always used was much too heavy to carry, as far as his cave, but he did take cast iron pots and pans, and some white enamel splatter ware, as he thought he might need.

In the barn was a long cast iron stove, rusty, and never used, it was called a box stove, because most stores seem to have one that they used to burn the wood from wooden crates or boxes that things were shipped in. It was a simple stove, for the simple life Old Hank, planned to live. And it was easy enough to get to the cave, on the small two wheeled cart Old Hank was using. In a few weeks, Old Hank, had moved everything he thought he'd need to live in his cave. He even took the door off the small house, and some wood gathered here and there.

He had made a front wall, and doorway to his new home. Old Hank, cut a round hole throw the wood walling, alongside the door's frame, and set up the tin chimney of his stove out through that. He knew it wasn't the best place for a fire to heat his cave in winter, but if he made it hot enough, it would warm enough of the cave to make it passable for the cold Adirondacks nights. But as the cook stove at the old homestead, was the only source of heat there, many a night water would freeze solid in a bucket inside the house, so Old Hank was used to the cold, in a way.

Old Hank, had his heavy gray woolen blankets from the war, his uniform, a canvas field shoulder bag, brass compass, first aid kit, tin mirror, and round identification tags that he always wore. A few more odds and ends, and his felt covered canteen, was everything he came home with.

Old Hank, made many trips to town before winter set in. *To town,* meant Speculator. A two-day walk going, and, sometimes a three day walk back, depending how much Old Hank bought, carrying whatever goods he needed.

On his first trip, he bought a hundred feet for rope to fix his bed. It didn't have a nice feather mattress any longer, but he would work on something before winter came on.

Dry goods are what he needed most, beans, flour, salt, baking soda, lard, soda crackers, sugar, coffee and tea, always in tins, so the mice didn't get to it. Soap too, but he knew baths would be as scarce, as in the war. Only in warm weather would he be able to wash up well in the stream.

Water was one of Old Hanks biggest concerns. Water kept well in the cave, the natural dampness at night meant little evaporation. A good stream ran not too far from his cave. He'd walk down to it just about every day. He had a small tin pot with a pail handle, hanging on a stout tree limb. To the pots handle, he had tied a length of string. He'd toss the pot into the water.   Slowly it would float down stream a bit, whereas, Old Hank, would pull the filling pot back towards himself, as he stood on the bank and bring it up to him, he'd fill the larger pail he had carried with him.

This was good for now, but he knew in the winter, he would be chopping holes in the ice to get to the water, or bringing home chunks of ice to melt for drinking water. He feared more a dry-spell, beside the stream, there was no water close by. He had a barrel for rain water. But this water was not good for drinking. This water was only to use in the garden, he planned to plant in the spring.

In the war, he was knee deep, and sometimes chest deep for days, in water unfit to drink. Now his greatest want might be water.

There were fish is this small stream, not over 6 inches or so. But many a hot summer day, Old Hank would sleepily settle himself down in the warm sun, his back against a log, and drop a line in the water. His fishing poll, a thin bamboo pole, was probably one of the only new things he bought for himself in a while, except for a small round tin of hooks and some line now and then.

He had a good supply of 22's for his Quackenbush rifle, and could always buy more. It was a gift to him from his father when he was eleven or so. He knew with it, he would always have meat, be it opossum or rabbit.

Old Hank, would take his army blanket, roll it up trump line fashion; that meant rolled tightly with a length of rope going through the middle of the roll, letting him carry it slung over one shoulder. He'd take some supplies with him in his field bag, a tin of beans, a tin of fish, some crackers and coffee. The only large items, a small but thick coffee pot, and enamel cup, hung from the strap of the field bag.

Old Hank ate nothing until he reached his resting place for the night, other than eating wild blackberries, and such as he walked along. Night came on quickly, by 4 pm the woods were getting dark fast. In warm dry weather, there wasn't much to worry about, a small fire on cleared ground, and a soft bed of dry long needle white pine, was more than anyone could ask for. If rain came on, it might mean spending a night sitting up, sleeping as you can, under a small rock ledge.

Old Hank, knew the woods well, he knew all the places to hold up however the weather turned out. Nothing brought more comfort to Old Hank, than once camp was made, to set a pot of dark coffee boiling. His coffee pot wasn't a fancy percolator any longer, it was just an old perk with a hinged top, its basket gone. Hank, would toss a hand full of coffee grounds in the pot, pour some water from his canteen in, and set it over a small fire. In no time the water would be boiling, and he'd have to move it so that it was set, just to simmer. There was something about the smell off coffee, and the scent of a pine forest, that made all the trials of life seem far away. Old Hank, would slowly pour the hot coffee into his white enamel cup, as not to get to many coffee grounds in it, but even if he did, they'd only settle to the bottom of his cup.

In the morning, as the sky was turning from black to dark blue, Old Hank would strike a match, and light the small twigs he had set under his coffee pot, just before going to sleep. He knew he would want a hot cup of coffee to start his day.

His blanket rolled, and strung again on the cordage, he tossed the heavy grounds from the pot, and hang it again from the strap of his field bag. By mid-day, Old Hank reached Speculator.

There was one dry-goods store in Speculator, that served as post office, town clerk's office, and hardware store. There was a blacksmith shop, an undertaker, a church and a few homes also. There was also a hotel, opened mostly from spring to early fall, that served, *the city folk,* as everyone called them.

They were the rich, who came to Speculator to get away from the city. They'd come to relax, and enjoy the fresh air of the mountains. Others came too, and hired guides to take them fishing, or deep into the Adirondacks, to hunting camps.

Old Hank, walked onto the wide porch of the dry-goods store, on its large dusty flat glass windows were painted with chipping gold letters that read Speculator Hardware. On the porch stood barrels with shovels, rakes and hoes sticking up from their open tops. A large spool of heavy rope was tucked between the barrels, and tinned pails some rusty, some new with bailed handles sat upside down as to keep rain water out.

The two tall thin doors of the shop stood open, mostly they were always opened, but there was a bell atop one of the doors that rang when you opened it. Old Hank, bought his usually supplies, flour, some sugar, coffee, candles, always candles, and more. Old Hank walked about the store just looking at everything.

Old Hanks grandfather, taught him a lot about the woods, what-to twigs to chew on when you had a headache, and what leaves to put on a bee sting, but still Old Hank looked at all the *patented medicines*. There were *elixirs* for this, and *compounds,* to cure that. Little pills for your liver, *purges,* and pills, *to cure man or beast!* Old Hank, took a small round tin, with an orange label of a black salve, his mother always called it, *drawing salve*. He also bought a little tin of powdered sulfur too. Behind a curved glass case, sat bottles of ink, next to slender wood pens, and small boxes of nibs. Old Hank thought about writing. He thought about writing about his time in the war. He thought about just writing about his life. And he thought about writing just about the big woods.

The Adirondacks were huge, impassable in places, with water falls and lakes tucked in places where few men ever set foot. He felt like telling the world about this land he loved. He thumbed a thick pad of white paper that sat on a counter, with envelopes and others things, fancy writing papers and envelopes, the type of things, *the city folk,* would buy and write back home with. Old Hank, walked away from the pen and paper, to a far corner of the store.

Here hung steel traps in every size to catch anything from muskrat to bear. Old Hank felt the pointed teeth of the large traps that would snap close onto a bare or wolfs leg.

No wonder some animals chewed their own foot off, there was no way one would be able to pull themselves out of that, Old Hank thought.

He then took one of the rifles from the wall. He worked the heavy bolt of the rifle, it clicked loudly making some in the store look over to him. He thought of the hundreds, if not thousands of times he did that in the war. He knew he should have a larger rifle than his Quackenbush 22, but he shook his head, *no not today,* and put the rifle back in the rack on the wall.

Next Old Hank, looked at the large pack baskets that stood on the floor. He picked it up and looked at its even weave. His grandfather had one like this he remembered. He'd sometimes let him carry it, how it thumped and bounced on his back. Old Hank, looked at the bottom of the basket, it had two wood runners, as not to sit on the ground when taken off, he liked that. He turned it right side up again, and looked at its canvas shoulder harness. Old Hank liked it a lot, he nodded yes to himself, and carried it to the counter. "That too, Hank?" said the shop's owner, who knew Hank well enough. "Yes," said Old Hank, taking silver coins from a pouch that hung from the belt at his waist. "That will be it?" asked the man, as Old Hank, set the coins on the dark counter top that was well worn from years of use.

Old Hank nodded yes, as he put what he perched into the weaved pack basket. Then he stopped. "Something else?" The shop owner asked. "Yes," said Old Hank. "A bottle of that ink, some pens and a box of nibs. And a pad of paper. But that will have to go on my account," said Old Hank. The man nodded, got the items Old Hank asked for, then pulled a long thin ledger from a shelf behind him, were he stood. "$1.20 next time in," said the man jotting what Old Hank bought in the ledger. Old Hank nodded yes.

The shop owner, then said, he'd wrap the tablet of paper in some butchers' paper, knowing Old Hank had a walk ahead of him, and that it might rain. Old Hank thanked him, and put the wrapped package into his field bag, rolling its strap around the canvas bag, and set that into the pack basket also.

Occasionally Old Hank, would walk down to the graves of his mother and father, down by the church. But not this time, sometimes he could, and sometimes he couldn't.

Old Hank, slipped the pack basket on, he adjusted the harness a few times, then walked off the planking of the dry good store, and headed back into the woods. At the end of the dirt road, Old Hank followed a trail not many would have even noticed. A little further on, and he could have just as easy never have been seen again.

Squirrels ran by the dozen over limbs of the trees, a woodpecker knocked on a dead trunk, and the ground was alive with scampering chipmunks. Before the woods early call of night, the blue sky had turned a steel gray, and droplets of rain quivered each leaf of the forest. Old Hank knew he'd better find *a place to night up,* as his grandfather called it. He hated stopping this early, but he knew the rain would only make the forest darker sooner. He knew of a small cave not far, maybe two or three miles, and so headed for that.

The cave, set up a steep hillside. He found the cave by chance on one of his trips to town, that time, a snow had fallen, and Old Hank wasn't looking forward to a

cold night of sleeping outside with only his blanket. He saw the footprints of a Lynx in the snow, they went up that steep hill, and Old Hank thought maybe that it was on its way to its den. Indeed, a Lynx had made a small cave its home, but as Old Hank approached it, the Lynx ran off. Old Hank approached the cave with the same care as he did that first time.
He knew that the Adirondacks had all kinds of animals, from bear to wolves, even mountain lion from time to time were seen. His grandfather had taught him a trick, of any cave he wanted to explore, first throw rocks into it. Most of the time, any animal, if in the cave would run out, if only to look about. And once empty, to build a fire at its entrance to keep what might be calling this his home, out! Old Hank, tossed a rock into the cave. He could hear it rattle on the stone floor.

He tossed a few more in, larger rocks, nothing came out. Old Hank, used this cave before, and knew it wasn't large, but it was more shelter than just a rock ledge, or settling down under a large fallen tree. The cave wasn't high enough to stand in, even sitting Old Hanks' head almost touched the top, but it tapered down to the back wall, so that if you laid down your head would be just a foot or so from the caves entrance. But at the further end, something had made its den.

In a bedding of leaves and twigs, was a putrid mass of hair, feathers and bones, the remains many of a meal. Old Hank knew, he wouldn't be going deep into the cave.

He made a quick small fire of leaf debris from the caves floor, and once going, added small wet twigs and small limbs that were in easy reach just outside the cave. Once the fire was going well, and his nights home protected, he would get larger wood, to last longer in the fire.

Old Hank, moved the pack basket deeper into the cave to keep it dry. He felt the canvas field bag, it felt damp, so he opened it, and felt the package wrapped in butchers' paper, it was dry to the touch. Old Hank was glad he had refilled his canteen from the hand pump at the store in town. He again filled his coffee pot, tossing in a hand full of coffee grounds, then rested his head against the pack basket, waiting for his coffee to boil. Old Hank, was more tired than he knew, for he awoke in total darkness, the rain was heavy. Old Hank could hear the rain, as he struck a match on the caves wall, and he looked about.

While asleep, the fire had boiled his coffee up and over the pot, putting the fire out. He brushed the wet cinders away, to started a new fire.

Old Hank pulled from the sheath that hung from his belt, his knife. It was an old Green River knife that he carried for years, even as a boy. The knife was about 8 inches long with a blade about an inch wide, with a tip that was more bulbous than pointed. There was many times he wished he had this knife with him while he was at war.

Old Hank, picked up a piece of dry branch that was on the caves floor. With the knife, he shaved off some kindling, and started another fire. There was still enough coffee in the pot to heat up again. When the coffee was hot this time, Old Hank removed it, and filled his splatter wear cup.

He kept the fire going, as he sat back, and looked at the blackness at the cave entrance. Rain curled its way under the top of the cave, and dripped to the floor, but didn't make Old Hank wet at all.

Out in the blackness, he could hear the angry cries. of what he knew must me the Lynx, angry because he lost his dry home, at lease for tonight.

Morning came clear, bright, and cool. Old Hank, again slept deep, and longer than he usually did. Rarely did the sun find him in bed.

At the cave's entrances, Old Hank saw a quick blur of blonde and black speckled fur. He smiled, knowing it was the Lynx, looking to see if it was free to come home again. Old Hank, chuckled a bit knowing that the Lynx would probably spend most of the day inside its cave licking himself dry from his night in the rain.

By the evening of the next day, Old Hank reached his home again. The entrance to the cave was 10 or 12 feet wide, and about 8 foot, at its highest point. The old wooden door stood slightly off center, to one side of it was the tin chimney of Old Hanks box stove.

To the other side, Old Hank, had built a small window, made from one he had taken from his home, on one of his last trips there. He knew that little house would soon fall into decay. The barns' roof for a while was sagging at its center and would be the first to fall.

The home would stand for a while. But with the door and window gone, it would become the home to animals in short time. It was still well stocked when he left it, rows and rows of canned vegetables stood on shelving in the kitchen. Old Hank, wished he could have taken all of them, but he knew being glass, many would break on the trip. He had taken a few, and when they were gone, that would be the last of a homemade meal he would ever have again. The flour in cloth sacks, would split in time. Sugar would be gone the first night to the mice, and raccoon. Of chairs, he knew he could make his own, but he wished he could have taken the round table, that when the top was lifted, made a bench type chair. Clothing too he knew someday he'd wish he took more of. A lot still hung from hooks. And his mother's hope chest, that his father would never open again once she had died, whatever clothing was in it, would make a warm home to forest friends, until that too, would split, and like a coffin of old, all would go back to the earth from which all comes.

Old Hank, pulled the string that protruded through his door that lifted a wooden latch on the inside. He push the door open, and walked into the darkness of the cave. Through the window came a little light, and he could see the candle he kept on a stone outcropping of the caves wall.

Old Hank, struck a match, and lit that

candle. The glow gave him, the light he needed to walk to the table and the two chairs he made. The salvaged wood, was nailed to two good sized sections of tree trunks he had rolled in after peeling the bark off as not to bring in bugs. The chairs, were branch and bramble, he had gathered. His hatchet cleaned the four-foot-high branches that made the backs of the chair, as likewise the shorter front legs. Some split wood, made the seat, while grape vines, dried but then soaked in water, made good cordage to fasten the chair together.

Old Hank tossed this rolled blanket onto the rope bed. He had made somewhat of a mattress out of two coarse horse blankets he had bought in town at one time. He could still feel the roping of the bed through the blankets, but it wasn't bad.

Old Hank, lit two candles that stood on the table in tin holders, then set his new pack basket on one of the chairs, and started taking the items out, laying them on the table. Old Hank, sat as he pulled from his field bag the wrapped package, and untied the twine.

He set the small bottle of ink aside, and took the wood pens that the shop owner had also wrapped. Old Hank, took the small box of nibs, and slid it open, the same as a matchbox. Old Hank, inserted one of the thin nibs in the tip of the wooden pen. The tablet of paper, was sewn into a brown card cover. For some reason, he felt the need to write his name on the stiff cover. He wiggled the cork from the top of the bottle of ink, then dipped the pen tip in, and lightly wiped the very tip of the nib on the glass mouth of the small bottle.

He was going to write William, but he thought it was so long that he was called that, that it didn't even seem like his name any more. In fine script he wrote Hank, then smiled to himself, and wrote the word, *Old* before it.

Old Hank, he said to himself, as he read the words in his mind.

**Evolve Today Publishing
Shelley Brienza**
Mayfield, NY
Email: sdigestpublishing@gmail.com

February 2021
Mayfield, NY
Printed in the U.S.A.
All rights reserved. This book may not be reproduced in whole or in part without prior permission from the publisher, except by a reviewer, who may quote brief passages in a review; nor may any part of this book be reproduced, stored in a retrieval system, or transmitted in any form, or by electronic, mechanical, photo-copying, recording, or other means, without prior permission from the publisher. Publisher will not be held liable for content within. All stories are the property of the author.

Made in the USA
Middletown, DE
27 July 2024